TRICK OR TREAT, LITTLE CRITTER®

BY
GINA AND MERCER MAYER

For Bill Pruden

A Random House PICTUREBACK® Book

Random House 🏠 New York

Trick or Treat, Little Critter book, characters, text, and images copyright © 2019 Mercer Mayer
Little Critter, Mercer Mayer's Little Critter, and Mercer Mayer's Little Critter and Logo are registered trademarks and
Little Critter Classics and Logo is a trademark of Orchard House Licensing Company. All rights reserved. Published in the
United States by Random House Children's Books, a division of Penguin Random House LLC, 1745 Broadway, New York, NY 10019,
and in Canada by Penguin Random House Canada Limited, Toronto. Originally published in slightly different form by
Golden Books, an imprint of Random House Children's Books, New York, in 1993.
Pictureback, Random House, and the Random House colophon are registered trademarks of
Penguin Random House LLC.

Visit us on the Web! rhcbooks.com • littlecritter.com

ISBN 978-1-9848-3071-5 (trade) — ISBN 978-1-9848-3072-2 (ebook)

MANUFACTURED IN CHINA

10 9 8 7 6 5 4 3 2 1

Halloween was coming.
We had a lot to do to get ready.

We went to the store to get our
costumes and Halloween candy.

There were Halloween
decorations everywhere.
We bought a glow-in-the-dark
skeleton for our front door.

There were lots of costumes. It was hard to choose. Dad picked out a creepy mask for himself.

My baby brother
didn't like the mask
very much.

So Dad chose a silly one instead.

My sister and I picked out a
bunny costume for our brother.
Mom said, "Maybe next year."

I tried on a cowboy costume . . .

a green
monster
costume . . .

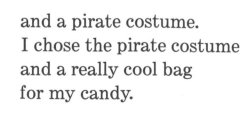

and a pirate costume.
I chose the pirate costume
and a really cool bag
for my candy.

My sister chose a princess costume.
I thought she looked silly. Dad said,
"She looks very pretty."

The next day we went to a farm to get a pumpkin. We rode to the field on a big hay truck. The hay made Dad sneeze a lot. I thought it was fun.

There were pumpkins
everywhere in the field.
I found the perfect one.
So did my sister.

We had to draw straws.

When we got home, we put
the pumpkin on the table
to make it into a jack-o'-lantern.
But when Dad started cutting,
my sister screamed, "Don't hurt
my pumpkin!"

Dad drew a face on
the pumpkin instead.
My sister said, "It looks cute."
I said, "It looks dumb."

On Halloween day we had
a party at school. We made
masks out of paper bags.

For the Halloween party, we had orange cupcakes and roasted pumpkin seeds and orange punch. Our teacher made a real jack-o'-lantern.

As soon as it got dark on Halloween night, my sister and I put on our costumes. Dad put his mask on, too.

Dad took us trick-or-treating.
The moon was spooky, and there
were ghosts and goblins everywhere.

I saw a lot of my friends. There were
some cool costumes. One of my friends
even had a costume just like mine.

At the last house on our block,
I noticed a hole in my candy bag.
Some of my stuff had fallen out.

I think my dog found it.

I started to cry. My sister said, "I'll
share some of my candy with you."

When we got home, we dumped all our candy on the floor and divided it up. Mom said, "I've never seen so much candy."

If I'm really careful, I bet I can make
my candy last all the way until next
Halloween. Well . . . maybe.